Tales from Ashanti Series 1:

Anansi and the Wisdom Pot

An African Folk Tale Book, set in the Culture and Traditions of the Ashantis in Ghana

Roselyn Byrne

Copyright © 2014 Roselyn Byrne

All rights reserved.

ISBN-10: 1499136757

ISBN-13: 978-1499136753

DEDICATION

To my Husband, Grandchildren and Great Grandchildren in United Kingdom, Zimbabwe, Ghana and elsewhere.

CONTENTS

ACKNOWLEDGMENTS	i
Chapter 1: INTRODUCTION	1
Chapter 2: PREPARATION FOR JOURNEY TO THE SKY GOD	3
Chapter 3: THE ANCESTRAL HAT WITH MAGICAL POWERS	6
Chapter 4: ENCOUNTER WITH THE GIANT BEES	8
Chapter 5: ANANSI BECOMES INVINCIBLE IN THE FORBIDDEN FOREST	10
Chapter 6: ENCOUNTER WITH THE OLD-WOMAN-OF-THE-RIVER	12
Chapter 7: ARRIVAL AT THE KINGDOM OF THE SKY GOD	15
Chapter 8: ANANSI GETS THE WISDOM POT FROM NYAME, THE SKY GOD	18
Chapter 9: THE RETURN JOURNEY HOME	20
Chapter 10: ANANSI TRIED TO STEAL ALL THE WISDOM IN THE WORLD	22
ABOUT THE AUTHOR	24

ACKNOWLEDGMENTS

Thanks to all my family, husband, grandchildren and everyone who helped in creating this book.

CHAPTER 1
INTRODUCTION

Once a long time ago, when the known world covered a small area and everyone walked to visit relatives, friends and to work, lived a half god, half human creature called Anansi. At that time too, people and animals could understand and talk to each other and they all lived side by side as neighbours, in a world of peace and harmony   Anansi, lived in a village called Kunsu in the Kingdom of Ashanti with his wife Asor and seven children, the youngest child is called Ntikuma. The main occupation was farming and the family worked together on their farm except for Anansi who is always wandering off for various adventures. Anansi is lucky to have a wife as Asor who does not complain about his idleness and always made sure that the work on the farm is done and runs the household with such efficiency. The family always ensures that Anansi and his exploits are protected and are always ready to come to his aid if he should find himself in a bind.

Anansi was known in the community to be a wise and clever but a cunning trickster who will do anything to do very little work and who also like to gain the upper hand in his dealings with all that he comes into contact with. His favourite past time is playing tricks and practical jokes on his friends. Sometimes, some of these tricks backfire on Anansi but it does not stop him from looking for the next victim. One person who has always been able to beat Anansi at his own game is, his son, Ntikuma and so Anansi is always looking over his shoulder to ensure that Ntikuma is not around before embarking on any of his pranks. However, Ntikuma is also always shadowing his father to find out what he is up to.

One day Anansi had an idea that if he had all the wisdom in the world, then he will be a rich man because everyone will have to come him to seek his advice on his or her problems. So, Anansi set out to prepare for a journey to obtain the pot, which contains all the wisdom in the world, from Nyame, the sky god, who is the owner and custodian of all the Wisdom of the world.

To reach the sky god one has to journey to a far-away land through obstacles, tests, intrigue and physical endurance to where the sky god lives on a tall mountain, which touches the skies. Anansi could not discuss his plans with anyone directly so he found a cunning way of getting information for his intended journey. He knew from stories heard about Nyame, the sky god that the journey to his kingdom is far and could be dangerous. There were specific customary rites and protocols to be observed for the journey and also to perform when one is granted audience with Nyame, the sky god. To overcome the risk of falling prey to the dangers on the way and to reduce the cost of travel to the kingdom of Nyame, the sky god, people travel in groups on pilgrimages. Anansi, however, could not or would not join any group for the journey because he intended to keep the purpose of his visit a secret from his family and the community as a whole.

So, Anansi went about in his own cunning way to gather information on what to bring on the journey and how to undertake the journey safely and successfully in acquiring all the wisdom in the world.

CHAPTER 2
PREPARATION FOR JOURNEY TO THE SKY GOD

Firstly, Anansi went to his cousin, Anokye, the chief high priest of the King of Ashanti and the Ashanti nation. Anansi and Anokye exchanged greetings and as custom dictates, Anansi was given a chair to sit down and a cold water to drink. Anokye then continued with the custom and told Anansi the state of affairs in his household, and proceeded to ask Anansi the purpose of his visit. Anansi answered, "Good day dear cousin, I come in peace and have no bad news to convey to you. I know that you are our great provider and protector of the spiritual needs of our great nation", Anokye nodded in agreement. Anansi continued. "It has occurred to me that Nyame, your father, has bestowed on you great mystical powers and ample number of years on this earth and you are going to be with us for a long time" Anokye nodded again. "Very few people have visited your father, the sky god, including myself, his oldest grandson. But I am now thinking of going to visit the sky god in his kingdom whilst I am still in my prime", Anansi lied, paused to see Anokye's reaction and then continued "I wonder what customary rites that one has to perform and protocol to observe, before one is allowed an audience with your father, Nyame, the sky god".

Anokye, the chief high priest replied. "It is good that you have made the decision to visit the sky god, a journey which is fraught with dangers but well worth with it for the benefits and blessings that one gets after such a visit. As tradition demands, anyone visiting an important person, and especially for a visit to Nyame, the sky god, one has to bring drinks, some of which are used to pour libation to say prayers to thank the gods for their protection; to pray to the ancestors for their continued protection in looking after the welfare of the clans; and to ward off evil spirits; before the visitor can state their reason for the audience with Nyame, the sky god".

Secondly, Anansi went to see Osono, the elephant, who was known to travel far and wide in the forests of the Ashanti nation. After exchanging greetings, Anansi started teasing and challenged Osono, the elephant. Anansi and said. "My dear brother, I am not quite sure when everyone praises you and say that you are the king of the forest and a great traveler who knows the forest like the back of your front leg". Anansi continued, "if it is true as they say, how can you describe the best route to take if one wanted to visit the kingdom of Nyame, the sky god". Osono, the elephant felt so insulted that he gave a complete description of two routes to take to the kingdom of Nyame, the sky god. One route was shorter but full of dangers and difficulties, including having to pass through the thick forest where it is forbidden for anyone to enter and where Mmoatia, the evil dwarfs live. The other route is longer but free of any problems and hassles.

From there, Anansi went to see Patuo, the Owl who was known to be wise and has extensive knowledge of the spirit world. Patuo, the Owl is also believed to have the power to foretell of any bad omen that is about to happen. "Good day, Patuo you wise old Owl", said Anansi. "I have come to consult you on a very important personal matter". Anansi continued. "Our ancestors of old have always consulted you as the all-seeing, all knowing, wise one who can foresee and foretell if there is an impending doom. Can you read my fortune for me as I have been having some strange dreams lately, but before that, can you tell me why it is forbidden for anyone to enter the 'forbidden forest'; … and what sort of dangers can one encounter if one goes into the forbidden forest?" Anansi knew that the Owl is not allowed to give such information to all and sundry. Patuo, the Owl refused to tell him. Anansi went on to persuade Patuo, the Owl, in his own cantankerous way saying: "There are rumours at the chief's palace that some elders doubt your powers as sooth seer. As you know, I have great influence at the chief's palace and also at the palace of the King of Ashanti. I am the only one who can persuade these elders to continue to believe in your powers of sooth saying, so in return for the favour that I am about to do for you, I think you should give me this information to convince me also that you are truly the all-knowing Patuo, the Owl indeed who has the powers of predicting doom".

Patuo, the Owl was worried that if the elders doubted his powers as a soothe seer, then, he will lose his position and respect within the community. So, Patuo, the Owl went on to describe and explain how the forbidden forest came to be and especially about the Mmoatia, the evil hairy dwarfs who live in the forest to protect and ensure that no one breaches the taboo. No unauthorized person has gone through the forest and returned to tell of their experience. The only people who are allowed to go into the forest are the Chief High Priest and the Chief responsible for keeping religious relics and rites for the King of Ashanti. Patuo added that any unauthorised person caught by the Mmoatia loses their soul which is taken out of their body turning the body into a 'zombie' used as a slave of the Mmoatia for the rest of their existence. The only other way that one can safely go through the forbidden forest is if one wears the ancestral hat with magical powers. The hat, which makes one invisible, has to be worn before one reaches the boundaries where the Mmoatia live so that one becomes invisible and is not seen by the Mmoatia. The hat has to be taken off immediately one passes the danger zone for one to become visible again. Patuo told Anansi not to touch anything else while he was wearing the hat because anything that he comes into contact with will also turn invincible. He also told him that on the way to Nyame's palace, he should look out for other spirits on the way, for some are good and helpful, but others too are bad and cantankerous and will do anything to hinder his progress on the journey.

Armed with all the information that he thinks that he needs, Anansi started his preparations secretly for the journey. As part of his preparations, Anansi came up with a plan. Every day, he will walk some distance and look for a secret place to hide food, drinks and other items that he will need for the journey. When Anansi had completed his preparations, he was confident and ready to undertake the journey. He knew the journey will not be easy but that even made him more determined to go as Anansi always enjoyed a challenge. He was even less worried about the Mmoatia, the evil dwarfs, now that he knows how to escape their trap and Anansi dismissed them as halt wits as he muttered to himself, "who in their right mind will prefer to live in a thick forest instead of living among others in the village". But Anansi knew that he had to get the ancestral hat with magical powers which is kept in the 'stool-room' in the palace of the King of Ashanti.

Ntikuma, his son, knowing how cunning and secretive the father is, started shadowing Anansi's movements. Ntikuma has seen that of late Anansi seemed to be pre-occupied and walk about with his hand under his chin as if in deep thought. After observing his father for some days, Ntikuma came to the conclusion that Anansi was planning one of his schemes and he was also determined to find out.

CHAPTER 3
THE ANCESTRAL HAT WITH MAGICAL POWERS

One fine morning Anansi said to his family that he was going on an important errand for the chief of Kunsu and will be away for a few days. He added that he could not tell them where he was going, because of the secrecy surrounding the errand that he was about to undertake for the chief of the village. To make things seem even more mysterious, Anansi told his family that the mission was so secretive that he will not be able to tell them the exact village, place or the message that he has been asked to convey. With no knowledge of the preparations that Anansi has already made for the journey, Asor, being the dutiful wife, prepared food and helped Anansi to pack things that he will need for the journey. Anansi bade farewell to his wife and children and set out for the land of Nyame, the sky god.

Anansi's confidence that he will be successful in his quest was boosted by his close relationships with the royal household, for, a few days before leaving for the journey, Anansi went to Kumasi to visit his spiritual godmother, M'sewaa, the Old Woman of the 'stool' house in the palace of the King of Ashanti. M'sewaa, is the keeper of the 'stool room' where such important ceremonial jewels, artefacts and relics for the Ashanti nation including the 'ancestral hat' with magical powers are kept. Anansi lied about the true reason why he came and told M'sewaa, the Old Woman that he was on a visit to see if she wanted any work done for her. M'sewaa, the Old Woman did not have any odd jobs for Anansi to do but insisted that Anansi should wait to be served food and drink before he departed from her house. M'sewaa went into the kitchen to prepare some food for Anansi and as soon as she was gone Anansi crept out and headed to the side of the palace complex where the 'stool room' was.

Anansi entered the stool room and went straight to where the 'ancestral hat' was kept. Anansi knows where to look for the hat because as part of his training in his youth as a 'pallbearer' at the palace of the King of Ashanti; he has seen the magical hat being used by the Chief High Priest during sacred ceremonies and festivals. Anansi took the ancestral hat with magical powers and hid it in his 'batakari' a rather loose and bulky smock garment, which he purposely wore for the visit to M'sewaa's house at the palace, so that he could conveniently hide the ancestral hat with the magical powers in it without being seen. After Anansi had eaten the food prepared by M'sewaa, he asked permission to leave with the ancestral hat hidden in his 'batakari'. Although Anansi intended to return the ancestral hat to the stool room on his return from the kingdom of the sky god, Anansi was aware of the enormity of the punishment that will be meted out to him if he was caught, but this also did not deter him from going through with his plans. Anansi walked through all the gates and checkpoints in the palace; greeting everyone he met with such enthusiasm and exaggerated bowing handshakes that his actions were even comical.

So, on the day that he had planned to start the journey, Anansi took with the ancestral hat; a gourd of palm wine and some bottles of the local gin to be used in pouring libation when he was in the presence of Nyame, the sky god. Anansi also took with him extra sandals; more food and water to supplement what he had already stored at vantage points on the way. Anansi also took some honey with him, his favourite food

Typical of Anansi, he was so confident that he would be able to gain the upper hand in any obstacles that came his way; he started whistling to himself as he went along. He felt even more confident of his success that he even started to talk to himself; mocking the unseen Mmoatia that he 'will be passing right in front of their eyes' and they will not see him because he was in possession of the ancestral hat with magical powers, which will make him invincible whilst he journeyed through the Mmoatia's camp in the forbidden forest.

Ntikuma, his son, who has been watching his father secretly for days, and knew of the amount of food that his father has stowed away along the path leading into the forbidden forest; knew that his father was up to no good. Ntikuma was even more curious to find out why his father wanted to enter the forbidden forest, so he tailed Anansi everywhere he went without Anansi's knowledge.

CHAPTER 4
ENCOUNTER WITH THE GIANT BEES

On the first day of the journey to the kingdom of the sky god, Anansi walked and walked until mid-day and came to a stop at one of the spots where he kept his food. He ate and laid down under a big mahogany tree to rest. Anansi started to dream of how rich he will be when he becomes the owner of the pot containing all the wisdom of the world. He dreamt about wearing the finest Kente cloth for himself and Asor, his wife, to the 'Addae Kese' festival to the admiration of all their neighbours. He also dreamt that, he was the owner of the finest and biggest house in the whole village, almost as big and beautiful as the Chief's palace.

Whilst enjoying how pleasant and enjoyable life could be for him and his family in the dream, Anansi was suddenly awoken by a loud buzzing noise. He opened his eyes and all around was a number of giant bees circling him. Anansi has had a few scrapes with the bees before because he has raided the bee hives a number of times and stolen the honey. So, when the bees were attracted by the scent of the honey that Anansi had in his bag, they knew that they have caught Anansi at last. "Hey Anansi, wake up" the bees buzzed. The bees were sure that Anansi had stolen the honey from their hive. "Where did you get the honey that you are hiding in your bag" the bees furiously quizzed Anansi. "Have you been stealing honey from our hives again?" "No" Anansi said. "I swear by the spirits of our ……" The bees cut him short and started tying him up with dried reed rope so that they can carry Anansi to their Chief for whatever punishment that will be meted out to him. "Please, let me explain ……", again the bees told Anansi to shut up and refused to listen to him.

No amount of denial and explanations were acceptable to the bees, they knew Anansi as a trickster and cunning being, who was lazy and will neither sow during planting time; nor reap during harvesting; and was always stealing food from others. They suspected Anansi was the culprit who had raided their hives for their honey on a number of occasions in the past and was always clever enough to get away. The bees have been looking for ways of catching Anansi red handed one day and thought that the day had come.

The bees took the honey from him and just as they were about to carry him off to the Chief of the bees, Anansi who is not easily defeated, came up with an idea. "Hey, fellows" Anansi said, "If I am able to prove to you where I bought the honey from, will you let me go free?" The bees fell about laughing, "when did Anansi buy anything when he can trick his way out to steal and get the thing for free", they said to each other, still not convinced that Anansi was telling the truth.

But the leader of the bees paused, thought about the double humiliation that Anansi will suffer if it turns out that he was lying about buying the honey. He convinced his mates and the bees agreed for Anansi to take them to the place where he bought the honey. Anansi took the bees back to his village but was extra careful not to be seen by his wife and children. Ntikuma, however, was following him all this time. Anansi brought the bees to the shop where he bought the honey and the village shopkeeper confirmed that he sold it to him. Feeling still suspicious of Anansi, the bees did not quite believe him that he bought the honey from the storekeeper. The bees knew that it was not difficult for Anansi to arrange with the village storekeeper to use him as his alibi, so before leaving, the bees took Anansi's honey with them anyway.

Anansi was furious because going back to his village meant that he has lost a day's trekking and the quantity of food has been reduced for the journey. He also learned that in negotiating with someone, you should always make sure that all conditions are covered, understood and agreed by all parties. The bees did not agree that they would return the honey to Anansi if he can prove that he was telling the truth. Anansi could not go home to sleep that night and had to sleep under a shed in someone's garden. Ntikuma did not sleep in the family house either because he could not risk losing the trail of his father and slept on a log nearby. Anansi set out again very early the next morning, followed by Ntikuma.

CHAPTER 5
ANANSI BECOMES INVINCIBLE IN THE FORBIDDEN FOREST

Anansi had already decided to take the short route through the forbidden forest to the Kingdom of the sky god. Even the threat of losing his soul; being turned into a 'zombie' and being reduced to an existence of eternal servitude to the Mmoatia, did not deter Anansi from going through the forbidden forest.

After two days of travelling, Anansi came to the big oak tree with branches stretching out to nearly half a mile. The Mmoatia's area of operation in the forbidden forest covered the area which is between this big oak tree with branches stretching out to nearly half a mile, going past the mausoleum where all the Kings, Queens and other royals are buried until you reach the big anthill that looks like a house. Going by what Patuo, the Owl said to him, before taking another step past the big oak tree, Anansi put on the ancestral hat with magical powers to make him invincible, as protection against the Mmoatia, the evil hairy dwarfs.

The Mmoatia are said to remove the souls from the bodies of anyone caught in the forbidden forest and the souls are kept in a big pot. The captured shell of the body, which is transformed into a 'zombie', is sent several feet down a mine where they are enslaved to work in the Mmoatia's secret goldmine. Ntikuma, who is as clever as his father had also worked out how he will cross that part of the forbidden forest without being seen by the Mmoatia. Anansi stopped to eat and rest for a while at the edge of the Mmoatia's camp in the forest and fell asleep after eating. Ntikuma quietly and carefully tied a thin long rope to Anansi's belt. So, when Anansi donned the hat and became invincible, so did Ntikuma and together they both continued on the journey. Anansi journeyed on until he reached the big anthill that looked like a house before taking off the ancestral hat with magical powers. Anansi and Ntikuma both became visible again and Anansi continued on unaware that Ntikuma was following him.

CHAPTER 6
ENCOUNTER WITH THE OLD-WOMAN-OF-THE-RIVER

Anansi continued on the journey for days until he came to a steep hill, which he had to climb as there was no other way to go round it. Coming down on the other side of the hill, he came to a river in a gorge. Sitting beside the banks of the river was a sweet old woman alone, and weeping in the middle of nowhere, looking pitiful and vulnerable at the same time. Out of breath from all the climbing up and down the hill, Anansi enquired, "Old woman, why are you so sad and weeping and all alone in this place?" "I am old and feeble and unable to cross this river on my own", answered the Old Woman. "Oh, come, let me help you. I will carry you to the other side of the river", Anansi offered.

Anansi hoisted the Old Woman onto his shoulders and waded through the river to the other side. When they arrived at the other side, Anansi stooped down and asked the Old Woman to climb down. The Old Woman wrapped her thin legs around Anansi's neck, choking him and refused to come down. Anansi pleaded and pleaded but the Old Woman will not climb down, she seemed to be glued to Anansi's shoulders.

Anansi continued to beg and used all his persuading and cunning talents to outwit the Old Woman but she will have none of it. For two days and two nights, the Old Woman sat on the shoulders of Anansi. When Anansi had the presence of mind to look around him, he could see bones scattered all around the riverbank. Presumably they were the skeletons of other victims of the Old Woman who had died from the same fate that Anansi was in now. Anansi was by this time tired and exhausted from hunger and lack of sleep and was even more desperate to find a way out of his present predicament. The thought of ending up as a pile of bones by the river left a lump in his throat. The next day Anansi, came up with an idea on how to get rid of the Old Woman on his shoulders.

"Old Woman", Anansi whispered in a weak croaky voice, "I am very hungry and thirsty and if I am to carry you around, I need my strength to do so, and I have to eat to maintain my strength. Unfortunately, I have left my food on the other side of the river, as I could carry you and all the food during the crossing, so could you come down as I go to collect this particular dish which I am sure you will enjoy.?", Anansi wailed. "I am sure you are also hungry and will like to join me in a feast of a delicious pot of yams and stew of beans and 'bosoa' cooked with all the seasonal spices", Anansi lied. 'Bosoa' is a variety of black pudding, a delicacy eaten by the Ashantis during festivals, and it is made from the blood of the sheep used for the sacrifice, and which are shared out to the various royal households.

The Old Woman was once a member of the royal household of Nyame, the sky god. She was exiled and banished from the palace because of her treachery and wickedness. Legend has it that in a race to see which of the sky god's wives will produce the firstborn child, the Old Woman caused the miscarriage of a number of the sky god's wives who became pregnant. Under the pretext of concern and care for the wellbeing of the mother and her unborn child, the Old Woman will prepare a concoction of herbs that she claims will help the mother and child to thrive. Of course the opposite happened in each case and all the pregnancies were aborted, except for one wife who was the Old Woman's favourite and accomplice making it possible for the favourite wife to became pregnant and bore the firstborn child for Nyame, the sky god. One day, during the observance of customary rites performed at the sky god's palace to 'outdoor' the ancestral stools and offer prayers and sacrifices to the ancestors, one of the priests went into a trance and started questioning and accusing the Old Woman of the part she played in causing the miscarriages of pregnancies of the other wives of Nyame, the sky god.

The Old Woman was brought before the sky god to answer the allegations but was unable to swear by the King's oath to prove her innocence and was found guilty as charged. As her punishment, she was banished and exiled to live in the valley by the river. Since coming to live in the gorge, the Old Woman of the River has used various forms of deceit and trickery to kill anyone who falls into her trap as revenge for her banishment.

The Old Woman pondered over Anansi's request and could not resist the offer of the sumptuous feast on 'bosoa', yams and stewed beans. She has not hand 'bosoa' for a long time and the thought of letting it go rancid and rotten by the time that she was able to kill Anansi was becoming hard for her to forgo. After a few hours of pleading and flattering from Anansi, the Old Woman agreed to climb down from Anansi's shoulders. As soon as the Old Woman came down from his shoulders, Anansi collected his bags and took to his heels. Then he remembered what Patuo, the Owl told him about not to trust anyone or anything that he came into contact with as some things in the forest and beyond are not what they seem to be and to be careful in his dealings with anyone on the way.

"Don't take things at its face value", Patuo, the Owl warned Anansi, "and don't take anybody or anything for granted". Anansi had forgotten to question the Old Woman at length as to how she came to be at that deserted place, he was only thinking of how clever he has been in reaching that point in the journey which he thought was only a few miles away to his goal. Anansi learned his lesson the hard way. He learned that by not heeding to advice, he nearly lost his life from starvation and strangulation from the Old Woman of the River. Because of his disobedience, Anansi also lost three days for the journey.

CHAPTER 7
ARRIVAL AT THE KINGDOM OF THE SKY GOD

On the thirteenth day, Anansi reached the outskirts of the Kingdom of Nyame, the sky god, after climbing a tall mountain, which took him two days to climb. Anansi noticed that on reaching the top of the mountain, there was no sky above or earth below him. They were all merged into one and in a distance he could see the tops of the sky god's palace. Anansi walked on until he came to a wide river that went round the magnificent palace. He has not seen a place as beautiful as the one that he was looking at. There were rows of houses neatly arranged in a row on both sides of the palace. The palace itself sat in the middle of the city towering over all the other buildings. The streets were smooth and shiny as if they were covered with some material that Anansi did not have a name. Trees were planted along the main street to the palace and on the last few yards where the road was wider, tall royal palms were planted on both sides of the road. For a moment Anansi was happy that he made the journey and offered a silent prayer to the ancestors for their protection and for making it possible for him to witness that such a beautiful place existed. He will have a lot to say to his wife, Asor and their children; and indeed to their neighbours.

Anansi was pondering how he would cross the river, as he could see no bridge, when a voice called out to him from nowhere. In the distance, he saw a man negotiating a canoe towards him. "Friend," the Ferryman addressed Anansi, "are you waiting to be ferried across the river to the palace of the sky god?" Legend has it that anyone with evil intentions will not see the Ferryman (although the Ferryman can see them) and will not be able to cross the river in order to enter the sky god's kingdom. Anansi wondered for a moment how the Ferryman appeared so suddenly but did not say anything; and when he gathered his wits about him, he nodded yes in reply to the Ferryman. "So, where is your payment for the crossing?"

inquired the Ferryman. Anansi had no money on him but noticed that the Ferryman had no sandals on and the idea came into his head that he could pay the Ferryman with the extra sandals that he brought. "Nana Ferryman" said Anansi," we heard in my village, Kunsu, which since the passing away of the last shoemaker for the sky god's kingdom, there was an acute shortage of the latest styles in sandals, so I brought these sandals as payment for you to take me across the river to the palace of the sky god". The Ferryman was delighted. He thanked Anansi profusely and offered to take Anansi on the return crossing free of charge.

The Ferryman asked Anansi what he had come to the kingdom to do of which Anansi informed him that he wanted to have a private audience with Nyame, the sky god, to ask for something that he thinks only the sky god can give to anyone. Anansi also told him of his encounter with the Old Lady of the River. The Ferryman told Anansi who the Old Lady of the River was and how she came to be alone by the river in the gorge. The Ferryman paused and asked how Anansi came to be by the route leading to the Old Woman which one can only reach it if one went through the forbidden forest, Anansi lied and said that he got lost along the way that was why he came to be on that side of the forest. The Ferryman was so touched by the offer of the sandals that he did not care to delve deeper into Anansi's answers and even volunteered to give Anansi some important information that he need for the rest of the journey. After narrating the story on how the Old Lady of the River happened to be living in such isolated spot in the forest, the Ferryman said to that Anansi was very lucky to be alive. He gave Anansi the name of the Chief Linguist and the address of where he lives, and told Anansi to see him first for quick access to Nyame, the sky god. He also told him that, the day was not a 'good day', for Nyame does not receive visitors every day. So, Anansi will have to wait for three days before he can see the sky god, if his request is successful. All of this information was very important to Anansi, who learned a lesson that "if you do good deeds, you are bound to reap the benefits somehow, some day".

At this stage of the journey, Ntikuma could not follow his father. Ntikuma also could see no other route to continue, so, as there was only one way in and out of the sky god's palace, he hid behind a tree and waited for Anansi.

CHAPTER 8
ANANSI GETS THE WISDOM POT FROM NYAME, THE SKY GOD

Although Anansi had taken the shorter route to the sky god's kingdom, he had spent fourteen days to get there for a journey that would have taken him seven days, because of the obstacles that came his way. He would have been better off to take the longer route, which would take the same amount of days, with no trouble at all.

When he reached the kingdom, Anansi went to see the Chief Linguist of the Sky God first as advised by the Ferryman which was also the custom, to tell him of his desire to seek an appointment for a private audience with Nyame, the sky god. The Chief Linguist agreed to enquire about a suitable day and time for him and took some of the drinks that Anansi has brought as a 'knock' to convey the message and seek permission for Anansi to see the sky god. Nyame, does not grant audience to receive visitors every day so it could be difficult to get an appointment to see him. Some days are set aside to pour special libation for the ancestors. Other days are set for special sacrifice and to give alms to the poor and the needy. One day in a week, Nyame holds public hearings where anyone with a grievance can come forward to present his or her case. Anansi, who is on a self-imposed secret mission could not use this channel to make his request in public. Even at these public sittings, protocol demands that the appellant speaks through the Chief Linguist, as no one is allowed to address Nyame, the sky god, directly. Anansi had to wait another three days before he was ushered into the presence of Nyame, the sky god for a private audience.

Addressing the Chief Linguist as was customary, Nyame, the sky god said, "Okyeame (linguist), inform my grandson, Anansi that all is well with us here in the kingdom, we have no bad news here, and even if it is bad news, with the help of the ancestors, we shall overcome them. Inform Anansi of anything that has happened here that he ought to know. Anansi has come to meet us in peace, he is the traveler visiting us and we are all here to listen to his reason for the visit". The Chief Linguist turned to Anansi and said, "Ohenena Anansi, you heard what Nyame, the sky god said, by the grace of the ancestors we have peace and nothing evil or bad has befallen us in the kingdom of the sky god; you have Nyame's permission to state your mission for your visit here today"

Before stating his case, Anansi produced the drinks that he brought and handed them over to the Chief Linguist as custom demands, telling him to inform Nyame, the sky god that, "Nana Nyame, the sky god, I bring a small token in the form of drinks, a small contribution to be used to pour libation and pray for us and the ancestors, and also to add to your stock so that if any of our people visit, it can be used to welcome them" The sky god indicated his acceptance of the offer of the drinks by waving his hand slightly and directed the Chief High Priest to open a bottle and pour the libation to pray for all who have assembled there, including Anansi. After the libation, all present were given small amounts to drink as was customary. When all the customary rites have been performed and tradition as well as protocols have been observed, Anansi proceeded to state his purpose for the visit through the Chief Linguist.

"Nana Nyame, by your grace, your protection over your people have made it possible for us to live in peace and prosper in the Ashanti nation", Anansi prayed, he continued. Your grandson (Anansi) has always observed all the customs and traditions of the land. I have discharged my work as a member of the local council at Kunsu with diligence. People have come from all corners of the Ashanti nation for advice and I have had to counsel and direct your people in matters of importance on many occasions. In order that I may be able to offer these services to your people in a more efficient way and eloquently, I have come to ask for all the wisdom in the world to be given to me", Anansi continued, "so that I will be properly equipped in the discharge of my duties in helping your people".

Nyame, the sky god was silent for a while, pondering over Anansi's request. After what seemed to Anansi to be a lifetime, Nyame gave his reply. "My grandson, what you are asking involves a lot of responsibility attached to it. I will give you the pot containing all the Wisdom of the world provided you promise to share it with all the peoples of the world". Anansi promised to do as Nyame has instructed him to do and collected the Wisdom Pot, he thanked Nyame, the sky god and asked for permission to leave. Permission was granted for him to depart and on his way out Anansi thanked everyone, shaking hands with the Chief Linguist, the Chief High Priest and all the Elders present. Anansi bid everyone goodbye and started the journey back to his village.

He came to the river where the Ferryman was waiting for him. True to his word, the Ferryman took Anansi to the other side of the river free of charge. Anansi said goodbye to the Ferryman after he asked him the direction for the other safe route, which does not go through the forbidden forest and of which he can take back to his village. Anansi has learned his lesson about taking the shorter route on his way to the sky god's palace. He was not prepared to risk losing the valuable cargo that he was carrying back home - the Wisdom Pot.

Ntikuma saw his father emerge from the ferry carrying a big black pot and wondered what was in it. He knew that he will by all means find out and will bid his time to look into the pot when Anansi was not around. Anansi took a different path for the journey home and Ntikuma continued to follow his father secretly.

CHAPTER 9
THE RETURN JOURNEY HOME

On the return journey home, Anansi kept looking into the pot and learned different things from it. The pot was full of wonderful ideas, knowledge and skills. Anansi started plans for how he will hide the pot out of the reach of his children; especially Ntikuma who Anansi knew was as clever and cunning as himself. Anansi was not so worried about his wife, Asor or the other children because they usually do not question him about where he has been; what he is doing, as Ntikuma who want to know everything that his father was doing. On this occasion though, Anansi was so happy that he has outsmarted his son, Ntikuma, who he thinks has no idea where he, Anansi was or what he was doing. Oh, if only Anansi knew.

On the way back, Anansi made sure that he passed through villages and towns that will be celebrating a festival or some anniversary. He always invited himself to these important celebrations, and gatherings where he knew a lot of people are assembled. Anansi always made himself known to the elders and asked to be included in the programme for the occasion and to be given a prominent place to sit at the high table with the elders. He will also demand to be introduced by his new self-appointed status as the keeper of all the Wisdom in the world. The people clapped and sang praises to Anansi on hearing of his new elevation in the society. At some of the gatherings, Anansi was able convince the elders to grant him permission to address the gathering, making a big play that he was available for consultation if anyone had a problem and needed advice about anything.

Anansi's activities and his behaviour on his journey back to his village were similar to a politician on campaign trip soliciting for votes. In all the introductions to the crowds and speeches were a good advertisement for Anansi, who consciously was soliciting for clients and to seek recommendations as a member for all the important committees, company boards and the traditional councils in the land.

When Ntikuma heard for the first time that his father was in possession of all the wisdom in the world, he was amazed, but as a dutiful and loyal son, did also joined in the clapping and shouted the praises of Anansi, his father. Ntikuma was even more resolved to gain possession of the pot for himself.

CHAPTER 10
ANANSI TRIED TO STEAL ALL THE WISDOM IN THE WORLD

Anansi could not hide how happy he was to secure the ownership of the Wisdom Pot, from Nyame, the sky god. He started calculating how much money he could make if he were to keep all the wisdom of the world to himself. Greedily Anansi muttered to himself, "I will not share the treasure of knowledge with all the people of the world. I will keep all the wisdom for myself".

So soon, Anansi has forgotten the promise that he made to Nyame, the sky god. He knew that if he intended to keep the existence of the pot and its contents a secret, then he could not keep the Wisdom Pot in his house. Anansi knows that it would not be long before his son, Ntikuma discovers the existence of the Wisdom Pot. Ntikuma on the other hand, was dying to find out the contents of the Wisdom Pot and to even steal it so that he could also learn what skills and tricks that he can learn from the pot, especially so that he will be able to beat his father Anansi at his own tricks and practical jokes. For days Anansi searched the woods and forests around the village looking for a suitable place to hide the Wisdom Pot. He was looking for a place that it will not be easy for anyone else to reach or even care to look for a pot.

Finally, he decided to hide the wisdom pot on top of the tallest tree in the forest not far from his house. Anansi took some vines and made a strong string and tied it firmly around the pot, leaving one end free. He then tied the loose end around his waist so that the pot hung in front of him. He then started to climb the tree but with no success after trying for a few times. He could not climb the tree because the wisdom pot kept getting in his way, bumping against his tummy.

Ntikuma, Anansi's son who has been following him secretly all this time, watched in fascination as his father struggled to climb up the tree with the pot. Finally, Ntikuma said, "Papa, if you tie the pot to your back, it will be easier to cling to the tree and climb." Anansi tied the pot to his back instead, and continued to climb the tree, with much more ease than before. When Anansi got to the top of the tree, he became angry, and thought to himself, "My youngest son, Ntikuma, with some common sense knows more than I, and I am supposed to be the owner of the wisdom pot containing all the wisdom in the world!"

In anger, Anansi threw down the pot of wisdom. The pot broke, and pieces of wisdom flew in every direction. People found the bits that were scattered everywhere, and if they wanted to, they could take some home to their families and friends. That is why to this day, no one person has ALL the world's wisdom. People everywhere share small pieces of it whenever they exchange ideas.

ABOUT THE AUTHOR

Roselyn Byrne
(a.k.a Nana Ama Serwaa Nyarko)

I was born into the Ashanti Royal family in Ghana and spent my childhood days between my father's Hia-stool house in Kumasi and my grandmother's house nearby. I always enjoyed accompanying my father each time that he took me to the palace of the King of Ashanti to perform his duties as Hiahene and especially to visit the late Queen-mother, Nana Ama Serwaa Nyarko I, whom I was named after. (At my christening I was given the name Roselyn which was the norm during the colonial days). I cherished the 'sixpence old coin' which the late Queen always gave to me during such visits, after she has advised me and I have promised to take my lessons seriously both at home and in school.

In the early 1970's I travelled to England to continue my education, qualifying as Chartered Secretary & Administrator and in between working full time, obtained an MSc degree in Charity Finance at the South Bank University.

My early childhood recollections centered on watching the observance of tradition, ceremonies, festivals and the performance of traditional dances. My maternal grandmother always gave advice for doing the right thing in life, by telling us an Anansi story. We always cherished the evening when we would gather around my grandmother in the open inner courtyard of her house to listen to her stories which mainly came from her repertoire of Anansi stories.

My debut novel in the 'Tales from Ashanti Series 1 – ANANSI AND THE WISDOM POT' is about how no one person can claim to have all the wisdom in the world. My version of this well-known tale, as it is in all my Tales from Ashanti series deals with the meaning of Ashanti traditional values, ceremonies and protocols and it is meant to explain, teach and educate the youth why certain traditions are performed and observed in the Ashanti nation. What Anansi had to go through on the journey to the palace of Nyame, the sky god to ask for the Wisdom Pot is filled with both captivating suspense and intrigue adventure.

My second novel 'ANANSI & THE SECRET GOLDMINE' is about Anansi volunteering to get rid of the Mmoatia, the evil dwarfs, who occupied the forbidden forest, terrorising and kidnapping villagers who are then used as slave labour for a secret goldmine operated by the Mmoatia. Anansi's method for destroying the Mmoatia is a unique stroke of bravery, so why did Anansi miss all the accolades and the glory in the end.

☐

Please visit Amazon retailer to discover other books by Roselyn Byrne:

Other books by this author.

Tales from Ashanti:
Book 1: Anansi and the Wisdom Pot.
Book 2: Anansi and the Secret. Goldmine.
Book 3: Anansi and the Magic Drum.

Printed in Great Britain
by Amazon